Sicky Vicky
and the
VOMIT COMET

Written by Lisa Regan

Illustrated by Pauline Reeves

BONNEY
PRESS

Published by Bonney Press
an imprint of Hinkler Books Pty Ltd
45–55 Fairchild Street
Heatherton Victoria 3202 Australia
www.hinkler.com

BONNEY
PRESS

© Hinkler Books Pty Ltd 2019

Author: Lisa Regan
Illustration: Pauline Reeves
Art Director: Paul Scott
Editorial: Zoe Antony

ISBN: 978 1 4889 1421 8

Printed and bound in China

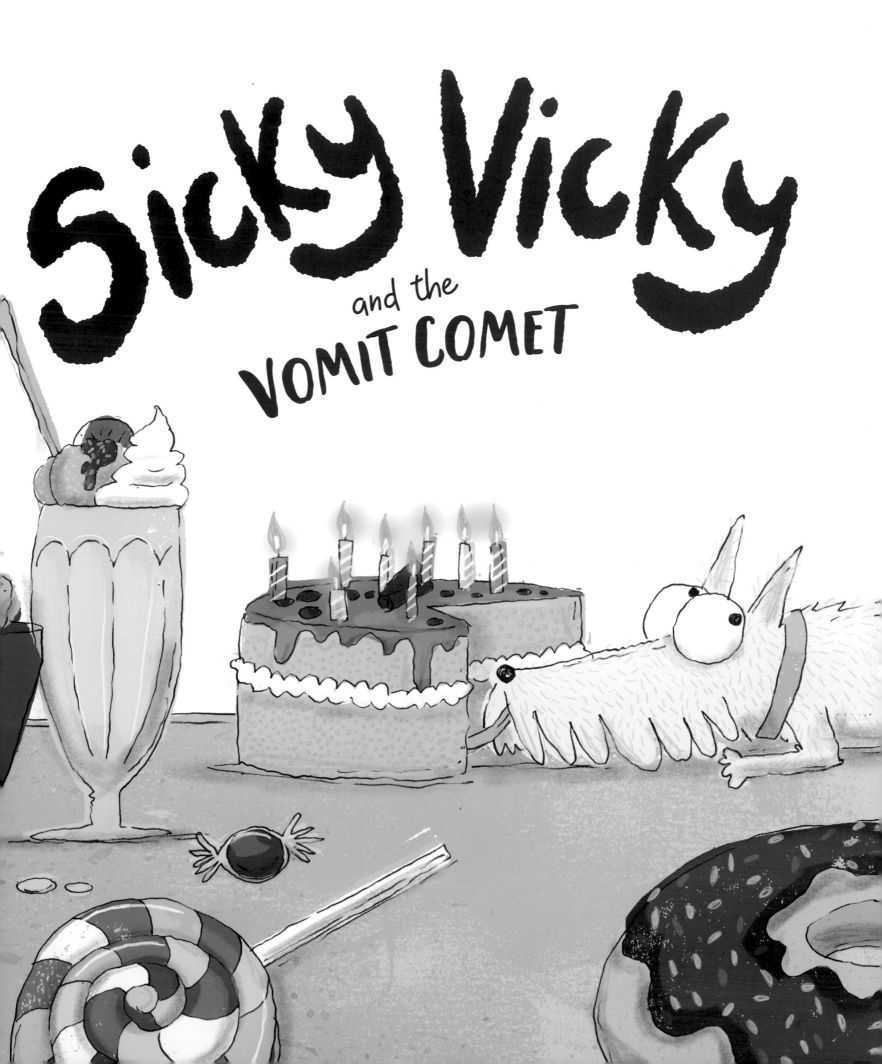

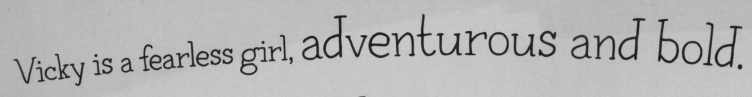

Vicky is a fearless girl, adventurous and bold.

Next week it's her birthday;
she's turning eight years old.

Mum says they should celebrate.

'What would you like to do?

Roller skating? Trampolines? A day trip to the zoo?'

But Vicky has a better plan –
to Hurley's Park they'll go!
She dreams of going on the rides that spin you to and fro.

Dad looks at her nervously.

'I don't know **how** you'll feel...'

'**Don't worry about me!**' she cries.

'**My stomach is like steel!**'

The big day comes and off they go. Her friends are all invited.
They meet outside and hurry in.
Vicky's ever so excited!

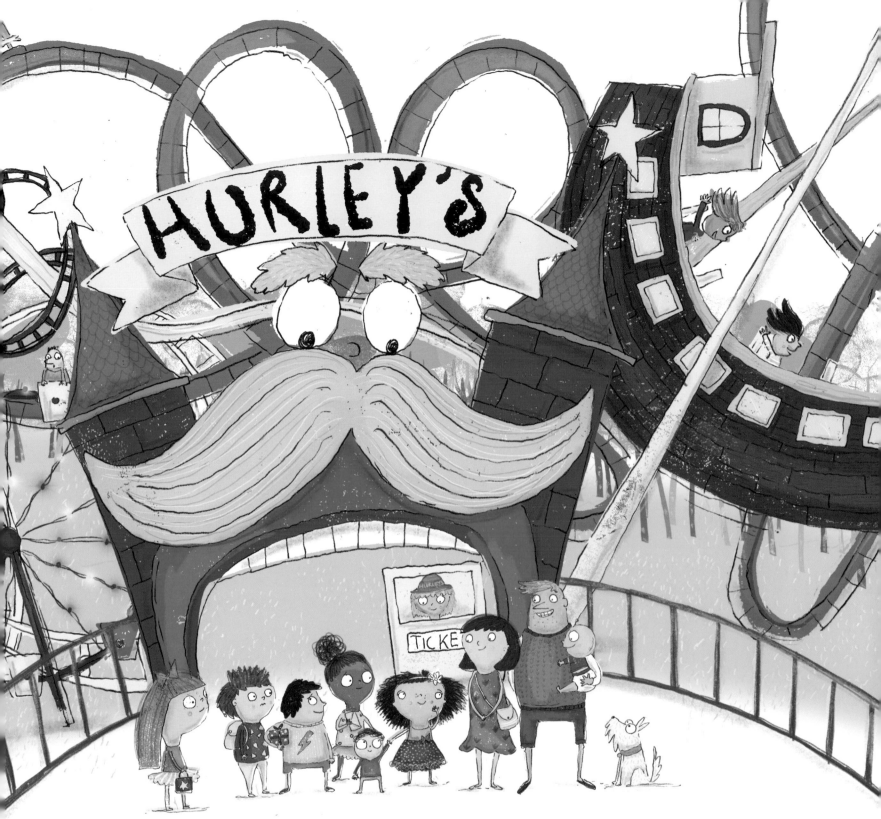

'I LOVE these rides! I don't get scared!'
she tells the party group.
'Fast ones, big ones, rides that twirl,
and those that loop the loop!'

Vicky slurps a giant drink and finds the popcorn stand.

'Let's ride the Waltzers first!'

she yells, grabbing Walter's hand.

Walter isn't keen at all. Spinning makes him sick.

'**Faster! Faster!**' Vicky screams.
'**It's best when it goes quick!**'

'Butterfingers!'

Vicky laughs, as she rides the Whirl with Claire.

She nearly drops her doughnuts as they're twisted through the air.

'**Woo hoo!**' she cries.
'**The Dragon ride! Danny, that's the best!**'

But as they hurtle
down the track,
Dan looks rather
stressed.

Then Jo appears at Vicky's side.
'Look – the mighty Comet!
That's my favourite ride of all.
Please say you'll come on it!'

The queue is long. They zigzag close, and gaze into the air.
People scream the whole way round.

It's REALLY high up there!

It's boarding time and Jo feels brave.

'Ready for a test?

Let's get seats right up the front. They will be the best!

'Close your eyes!' shouts Vicky.
'Pretend that you can fly!'
They throw their arms up in the air as they climb towards the sky.

Up and up and up they go,
then plummet to the ground.
Vicky's stomach starts to flip as they
twist all around.

'Make it stop!'

she whimpers as her face turns very grey,

Vicky's now regretting that she's stuffed her face all day.

The final climb is just too much.

As Jo admires the view,

Vicky tries to hold it in, but there's nothing she can do.

The screams of those behind her peak as faster they all twirl.

But the squeals get even louder still when

Vicky starts to hurl...

Vicky volcanically vomits.
She really makes her mark,

As the Comet zooms her spewy self all around the park.

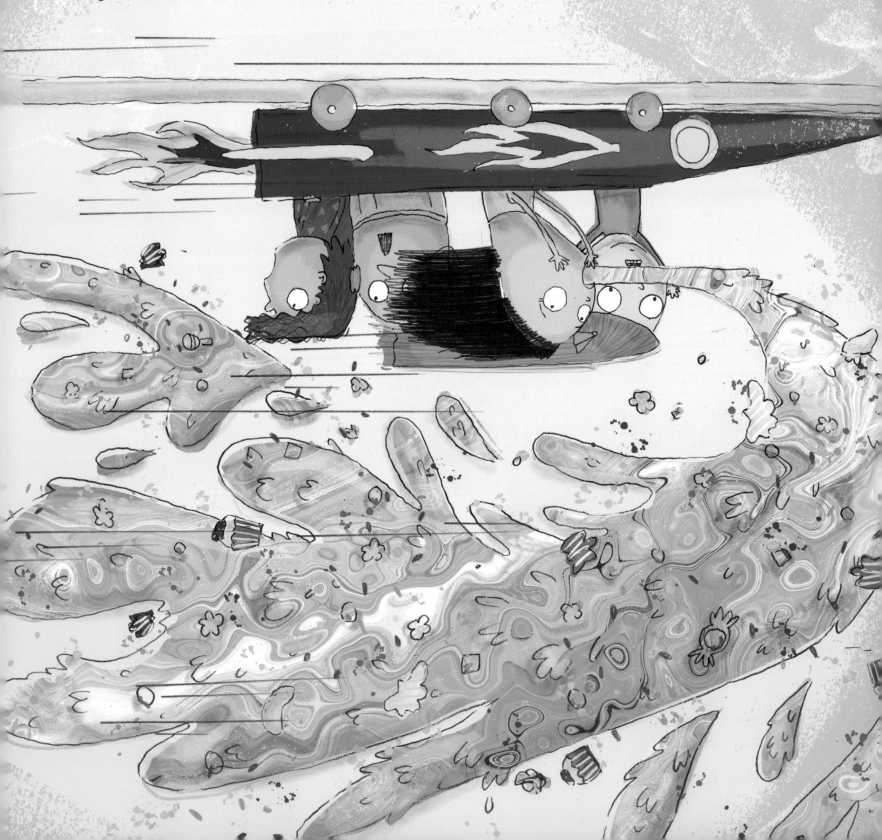

Inside the Hall of Mirrors, utter chaos is reflected...

and families at the Lucky Dip
grab something unexpected.

Couples in the Love-Train queue are suddenly rejected.

While riders on the Ghost Train witness
horrors unsuspected...

The Whack-a-Mole contestants score in a way that's
quite obscene.

Disastrously, the slide becomes a
gross spew-nami scene.

The people driving fun cars cannot dodge the sticky stream.

And the wave shows the most muscle
at the Test-Your-Strength machine!

Vicky staggers off the ride and
clutches at her tummy.

As her parents clean her up, she groans,
'I'm sorry, Mummy.

**No longer will I boast about my unbeatable belly.
I know now one too many twists
and it'll turn to jelly.**

I'll be more thoughtful of my friends and
always stop to think,
And I promise not to gorge again
on too much food and drink.'

Her soggy parents smile and nod: 'There's no need for rebuke.
A lesson learned – perhaps it was a blessing of a puke!'

As all the children head for home, Mummy hands out a treat.

Vicky just can't help herself...

'Perhaps just one small sweet...'